MW00942374

Dedicated to my dear husband, John,
and my boys, Adam and Levi

and all the kids I have taught over the years
who daily inspire me. Kids at...

The Friendship House - Billings, Montana

Camp Ihduhapi - Loretto, Minnesota

Geneva Glen Camp - Indian Hills, Colorado

Sunshine Acres Preschool, Hillcrest and Woodlawn
Elementary Schools - Lawrence, Kansas

Grace Lutheran School - Pocatello, Idaho

Once upon a time, in a very green wood,
under a very red rose, lived a fairy.

She was no ordinary fairy...
      Is there such a thing?

She was a Color Fairy.

      She created a rainbow
      of color wherever she went.

One day while napping on a very purple pansy, she heard a very loud sound.

She looked up and there was a very large, white wheel rolling by. She decided to follow it and see where it was going.

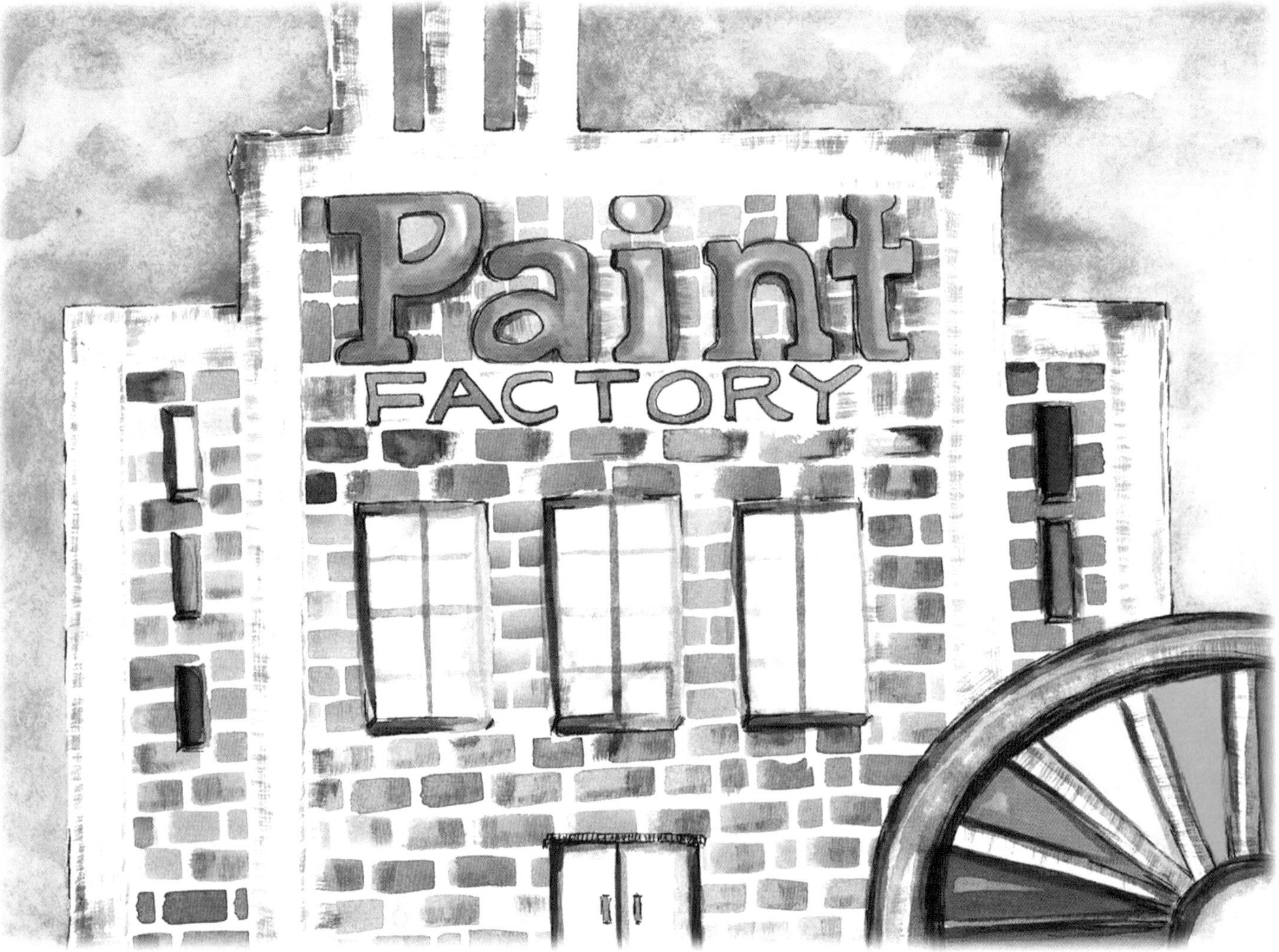
Paint
FACTORY

The wheel stopped in front of a very big, white building.

On the top of the building were very orange letters that read, "Paint Factory."

The Color Fairy was curious, so she peeked in a window. At a very brown desk, there sat a very white-looking man. He had white hair, a white jacket, and a white mustache.

The Color Fairy tapped on the glass. The white-looking man came to the window and opened it.

"Hello," said the Color Fairy in her very small voice. "I'm the Color Fairy. Who are you?" The white-looking man replied, "I'm Professor Paint. I own this factory. And I'm afraid I've never heard of such a thing as a Color Fairy." The Color Fairy answered, "Well, I've never heard of a factory before."

"A factory is a place where things are made in mass quantities," said the Professor. "And in this factory, we make paint...in many colors." The Color Fairy was delighted. She said, "That's what I do! But I'm not a factory, I'm a fairy."

Sell your books at
sellbackyourBook.com!
Go to sellbackyourBook.com
and get an instant price
quote. We even pay the
shipping - see what your old
books are worth today!

Inspected By: Santiago_Torres

00048070234

0234 s

0004807

The Professor studied the little lady and slowly said, "You might be able to help me. I just can't get the color right for spring grass. I have 7 1/4 parts of blue and 16 7/8 of yellow.

The Color Fairy waved her wand and said, "You need a sprinkle of blueberry and a pinch of sunshine."

And the green WAS very springy! The Professor
was astonished. "How did you do that?"

The Color Fairy shrugged. "I can't really explain."

The Professor professed, "Everything can be
explained."

The Color Fairy pondered, "Some things can...but some things can't. How can you make pink as enormous as a sunset?"

"How can you make blue as changing as the ocean?"

"How can you make indigo as brilliant as a peacock?"

The Professor had been
busily punching numbers
into a calculator trying to keep up.

"Wait! I've almost got it!" he said.

The Color Fairy pondered again...

"Some things you can't get...

but you can still enjoy...

Pointing to a jar of paint on a shelf, she said, "I think you've got that pumpkin color down perfectly."

The Professor said, "Thanks. Can I buy you a cup of coffee? I need advice on a new latte color."

This was the beginning of a long, colorful friendship.

The end...

of the book, but not the story or
the friendship or the explanations.

Lana Gribas lives in Pocatello, Idaho.
She has been an art educator for over
20 years.

The Color Fairy
is a character
created to teach
kindergarteners
the magic of
color mixing.

46894726R00020

Made in the USA
Lexington, KY
19 November 2015